Rabén & Sjögren Bokförlag, Stockholm
www.raben.se

Originally published in Sweden by Eriksson & Lindgren under the title *Fia och djuren*
Copyright © 2007 by Catarina Kruusval
Library of Congress Control Number: 2007930254
Printed in Denmark
First American edition, 2008

ISBN-13: 978-91-29-66836-0
ISBN-10: 91-29-66836-0

Catarina Kruusval

# Franny's Friends

Translated by Joan Sandin

**R&S BOOKS**

Stockholm  New York  London  Adelaide  Toronto

Franny has seven friends:
Croakie Crow,
Barry Bear,
Honey Bunny,
Ginger Giraffe,
Dashie Doggy,
Little Heddy Hedgehog,
and Itty Bitty Kitty.
Franny plays with her friends
every day.

One sunny morning Franny says,
"Get up, everybody! We're going on an outing."

But first she dresses Croakie Crow, Barry, Little Heddy, Honey, Ginger, Dashie, and Itty Bitty Kitty.

Then they all
go down the stairs.
"I'll go first," says Franny.
All the others follow:
Dashie,
Barry,
Ginger,
Croakie Crow,
Honey,
Little Heddy,
and Itty Bitty Kitty.

Then they all go down the path.
"Shall I go first?" asks Ginger.
"No, I'm the one who goes first," says Franny.
After Franny comes Ginger, then Croakie Crow, and
Barry, and Dashie, and Little Heddy, and Honey.
Last of all is Itty Bitty Kitty.

"Here we are," says Franny. "This is where we'll have our picnic. Here's a bun for Barry, a bun for Ginger, a bun for Honey, a bun for Croakie Crow, a bun for Dashie, a bun for Little Heddy. Did everybody get a bun?"

No, there's still one bun left after Franny has
taken hers. Whose is it?
Oh! Barry Bear is sitting on Itty Bitty Kitty,
and Itty Bitty Kitty doesn't have a bun.

Franny helps Itty Bitty Kitty.

Then Franny gives everybody
some juice in pretty little cups.

When everyone has finished eating,
Franny says, "Now we'll go on an
expedition."
First they go up the steep hill . . .

. . . and then they run
down the steep hill.

But they go too fast!
Little Heddy and Itty Bitty Kitty stumble
and roll and roll . . .

Uh-oh! Down into a hole!
"Help!" shouts Little Heddy.
"Help!" shouts Itty Bitty Kitty.
But no one hears Little Heddy
or Itty Bitty Kitty.

The others just run and run and run.
Look at them! They don't even notice that Itty Bitty
Kitty and Little Heddy have disappeared into a hole.

They all fall down in the tall grass.
They are so very, very tired.
They just lie there looking up at the clouds.

When they have finished resting, Franny says,
"Now the outing is over. It's time to go home!
Is everybody here?"
Franny counts them. There is Barry, and there is
Ginger, and there is Dashie, and there is Honey,
and there is Croakie Crow, and . . . !
Where is Little Heddy?
And where is Itty Bitty Kitty?

They search in the grass.
But there's no Little Heddy, and no Itty Bitty Kitty.

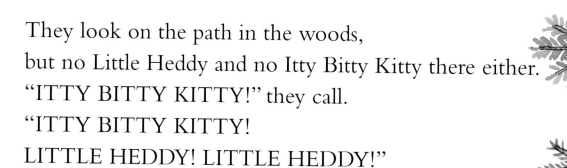

They look on the path in the woods,
but no Little Heddy and no Itty Bitty Kitty there either.
"ITTY BITTY KITTY!" they call.
"ITTY BITTY KITTY!
LITTLE HEDDY! LITTLE HEDDY!"
"Here we are!" comes a voice from somewhere.

"HERE!"
What luck. It's Little Heddy
and Itty Bitty Kitty!

Franny pulls Itty Bitty Kitty and Little Heddy
up out of the hole.

Then they all go home. They go up the steep hill.
And they go down the steep hill.
Ginger goes first, and then comes Croakie Crow,
Dashie, and Itty Bitty Kitty . . .